NOTE TO PARENTS

Based on the beloved Walt Disney motion picture *Cinderella*, this book expands on Cinderella's relationship with her animal friends. Although she is always busy with her chores, Cinderella takes the time to help the animals when they are in trouble, and she makes a special effort to understand their thoughts and feelings.

When it looks like poor Cinderella won't have time to fix up her old dress for the Royal Ball, her animal friends decide to repay her for all the kindness she has shown them. They learn what Cinderella has always known—that the reward of kindness is the happiness it gives others.

This book recounts one memorable episode from the movie that will help children learn an important lesson about the value of kindness. For the complete story of *Walt Disney's Cinderella*, look for these other Golden Books:

2456-32 WALT DISNEY's CINDERELLA
         (A Golden Tell-A-Tale® Book)

103-57   WALT DISNEY's CINDERELLA
         (A Little Golden Book®)

10056   WALT DISNEY's CINDERELLA
         (A Golden Super Shape Book™)

10200   WALT DISNEY's CINDERELLA

15546   THE NEW WALT DISNEY TREASURY

17865   A TREASURY OF DISNEY LITTLE GOLDEN BOOKS

Walt Disney's
Cinderella
and Her Animal Friends

A BOOK ABOUT KINDNESS

A GOLDEN BOOK • NEW YORK
Western Publishing Company, Inc., Racine, Wisconsin 53404

Once upon a time there lived a pretty girl named Cinderella. Cinderella lived in a big old house where she had to do all the chores. It was a lot of hard work, but Cinderella had her animal friends to keep her company.

She was so good, kind, and gentle that even the mice were not afraid of her. In fact, the mice came to her for help when they were in trouble.

One day a little mouse named Jaq scampered up to Cinderella. "Lew nouse gawt ginna rap flap!" he stammered excitedly.

Cinderella knew what he meant—that a new mouse was caught in the rat trap.

Cinderella ran to rescue the mouse. She lifted him gently out of the trap.

Cinderella called the mouse Gus. She gave him a tiny sweater and tiny shoes and a tiny cap to wear. She warned him about Lucifer, the mean cat.

Cinderella didn't like Lucifer, but she was kind to him anyway. She even patted his head when she gave him his breakfast.

Bruno the dog didn't like Lucifer, and he had plenty of good reasons.

When Lucifer wasn't eating out of Bruno's dish...

or chasing the mice...

or scaring the chickens...

he was getting Bruno in trouble.

Cinderella warned Bruno not to chase Lucifer. "We should all try to get along together," she said. "Remember, if you're angry, you can always just walk away." Her gentle voice and good advice soothed the angry dog.

Cinderella stepped outside to feed the chickens. She sang as she scattered the corn. The mice came to gather stray kernels and to join in the song.

Then Cinderella went to the barn to feed the old horse.
"I don't know why you bother with an old workhorse
like me," the horse whinnied.

Cinderella brushed his coat and combed his mane. "An
old workhorse? Why, just look at yourself," she said,
holding up the shiny bucket.

The horse saw his reflection. His chest swelled with
pride. "Thank you for caring about me, Cinderella. You're a
kind friend."

Later that day, a letter from the king arrived. It said:

> Tonight at the palace
> there will be a ball
> in honor of His Highness,
> the Prince.
> By Royal Command,
> all unmarried young ladies
> in the Kingdom
> are asked to attend.

Cinderella could hardly believe it—a ball, at the palace, for the prince. It was a dream come true!

She ran upstairs to get out her best dress. It was plain and old-fashioned, but with a ribbon here and a piece of lace there, it would look fine.

Yet Cinderella would not have time to fix it up until all her work was done.

Cinderella worked harder than she ever had before. But each time she turned around there was more to do. She had to—

do the laundry...

wash the windows...

clean the chimneys....

And on it went.

Cinderella's animal friends saw what was happening. Jaq called them all together and said, "Cinderelly always kind to us. Now we be kind to her."

The other animals agreed, and they came up with a plan.

Cinderella tried her best to get all the work done. All the while she wondered where her animal friends were. She missed their cheerful songs and chatter.

Cinderella was too busy to see that they were all around her, gathering scraps of ribbon, beads, and lace—*and* running from Lucifer!

Finally Cinderella finished all her chores. But it was already time to leave for the ball, and she hadn't even started to fix her dress.

After all that work, it was hopeless—she'd never be able to go to the ball.

Cinderella ran up to her room. She went straight to her window and gazed longingly toward the palace.

Suddenly a tiny voice called, "Look, Cinderelly!"

Cinderella turned around.

"Surprise!" sang a chorus of Cinderella's friends.

While Cinderella had been busy her friends had fixed up her dress with a pretty sash, ribbons, and bows.

They had stitched and sewn, and finished just in time.

"My dress!" Cinderella gasped. "It's beautiful!"

"We knew you wouldn't have time to fix it yourself," said a bird.

"We want to help," Gus said shyly.

"Try on!" Jaq urged.

Cinderella put on her dress. It was so pretty she hardly recognized it.

"What kind friends I have!" Cinderella exclaimed.

"That's because you're such a kind friend to us," the animals replied.

Now Cinderella was really ready to go to the ball and dance with the handsome prince!